W9-AMU-401

Plate 1: Santa Claus

Plate 2: Santa's Elf

Plate 3: Mrs. Claus

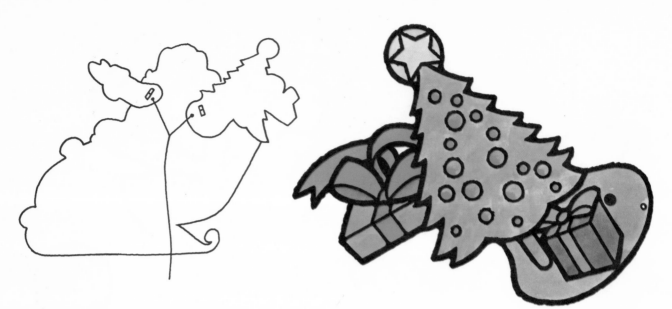

Plate 4: Santa on His Sleigh

Plate 5: Riding a Reindeer

Plate 6: Christmas Tree with Presents and Pets

Plate 7: Holly and Bells

Plate 8: Angel

Plate 9: Christmas Stocking

Plate 10: Christmas Mouse

Plate 11: Christmas Doll

Plate 12: Snowman